Short "o" and Long "o"
Play a Game

Library of Congress Cataloging-in-Publication Data
Moncure, Jane Belk.
Short "o" and Long "o" play a game / by Jane Belk Moncure ; illustrated by Norman Young.
p. cm.
Summary: Short o and Long o introduce the long and short "o" sounds.
ISBN 1-56766-931-X (library bound)
[1. English language—Vowels—Fiction.]   I. Young, N. (Norman), ill. II. Title.
PZ7.M739 Sh 2001
[E]—dc21
00-010851

Short "o"
and Long "o"
Play a Game

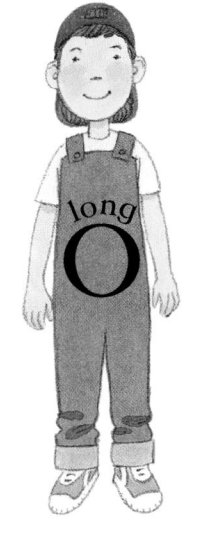

Jane Belk Moncure
illustrated by Norman Young

This is . He has a special sound.

Ox begins with his short "o" sound.

So does 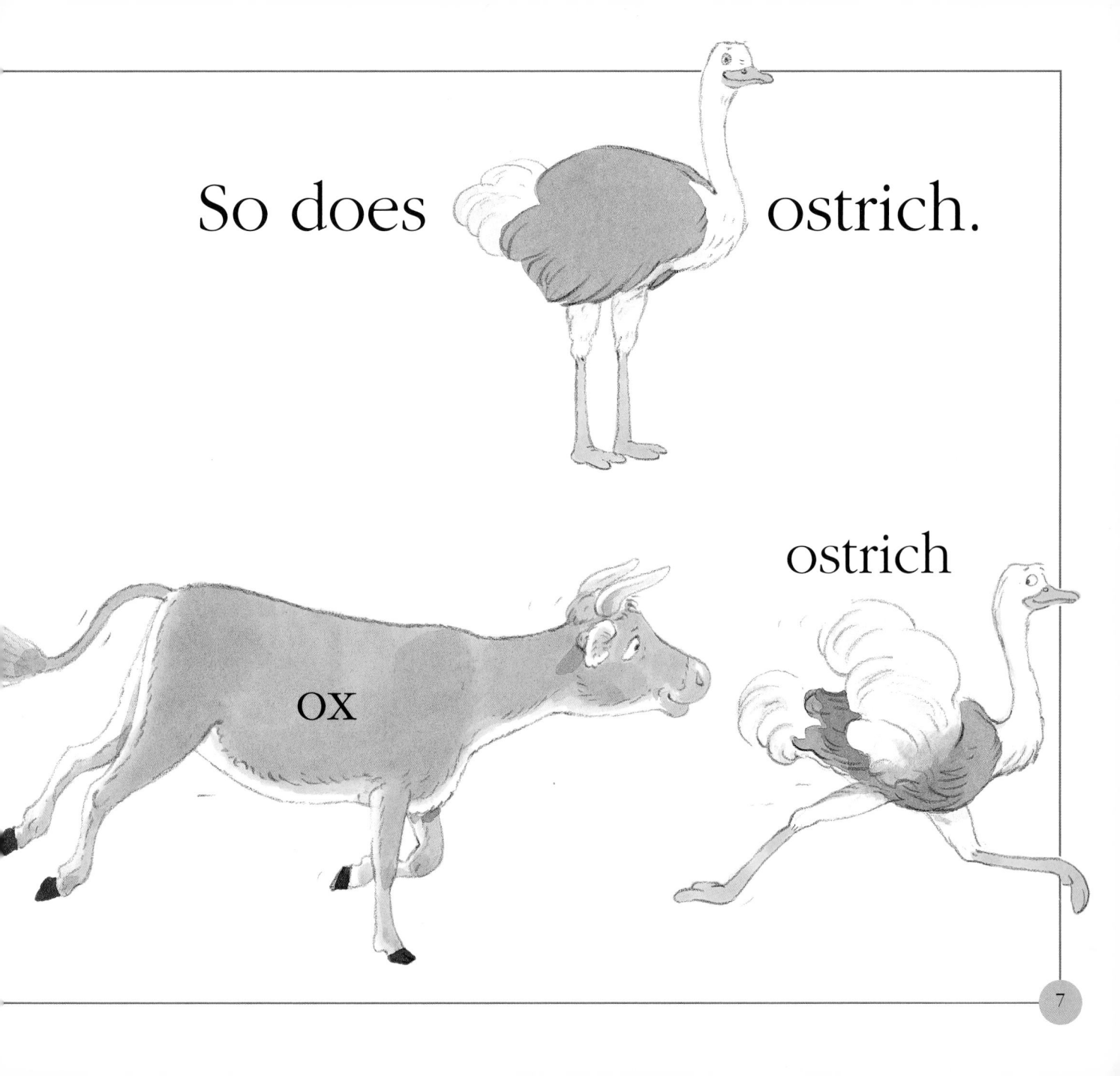 ostrich.

ostrich

ox

This is . She has a different sound.

Overalls

begins with her long "o" sound.

So does oboe.

Can you hear the  short **O**

and the long **O** sounds?

ox

ostrich

One day, Short "o" said,
"Let's play a game. I will
look for my sound in words.

overalls

oboe

long O

You can look for your sound
in words. We'll see who can
find the most words."

Short O found an octopus...

12

and an otter.

"I will win!" he said.

Long **O** found some

oatmeal,

an oak,

and some

okra.

"No! I will win!"
she said.

overalls

oak

oboe

Long O

okra

oatmeal

counted. "I win," she said.
"I have the most words."

ostrich

octopus

otter

ox

Short **O** counted. "No! No! No!" he said.

"I will use my 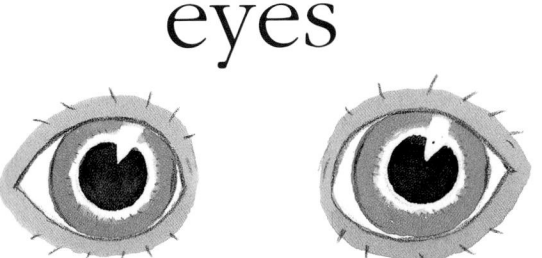 eyes

 and 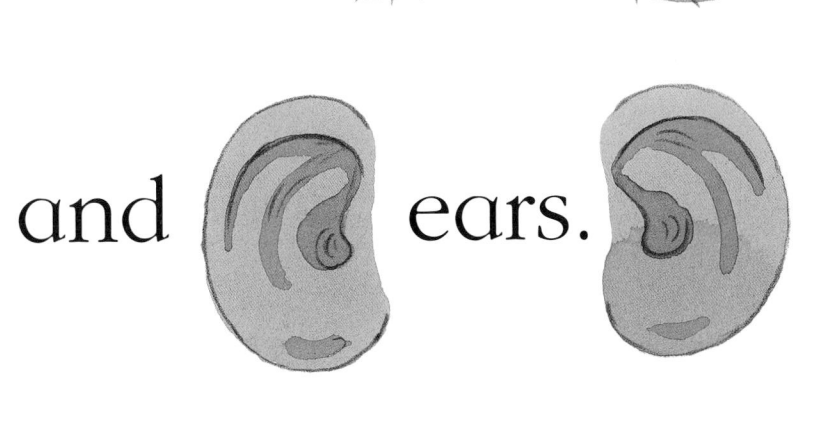 ears.

My sound hides in words. I will find words with my sound in the middle of them."

Short O found

a fox

and some rocks.

Then he found

a mop,

a top,

a pot,

and blocks…

lots of blocks.

"Now I will win!" said short O.

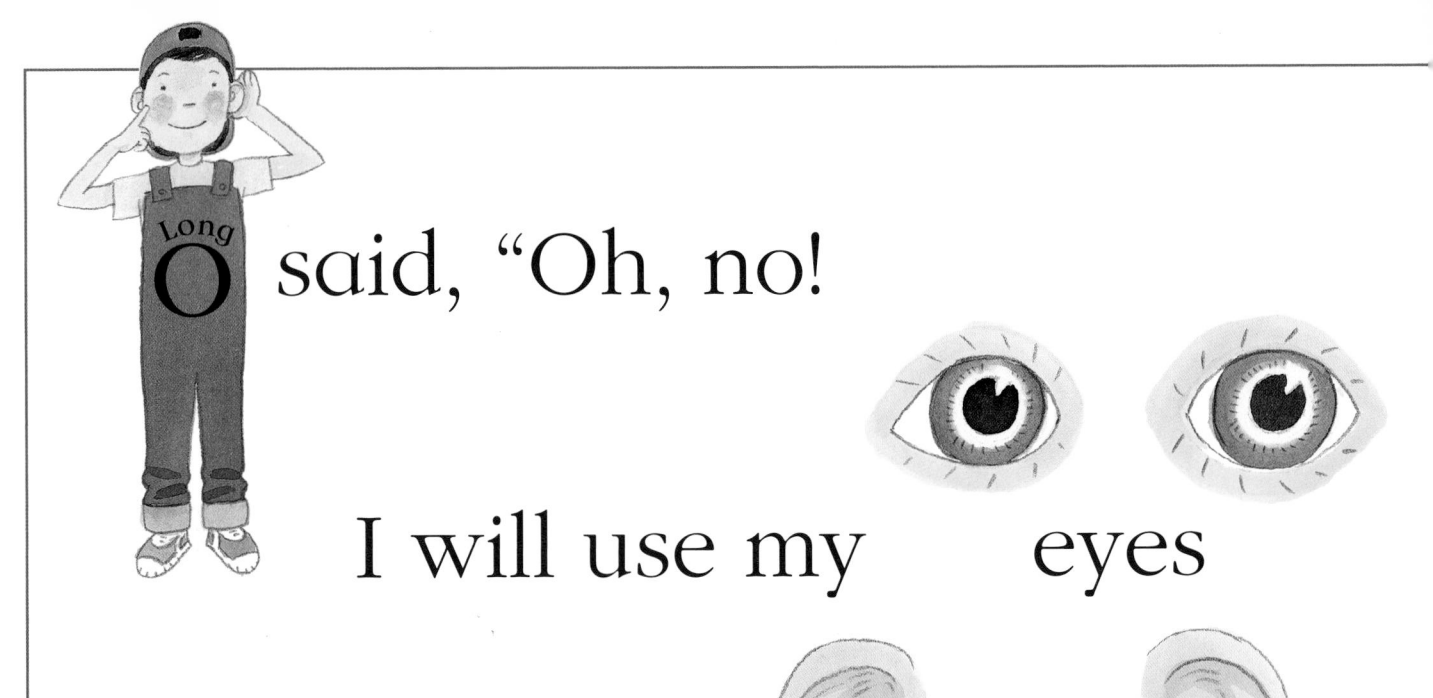

Long **O** said, "Oh, no!

I will use my eyes

and ears.

My sound hides in words, too.
I will find words with my
sound in the middle of them."

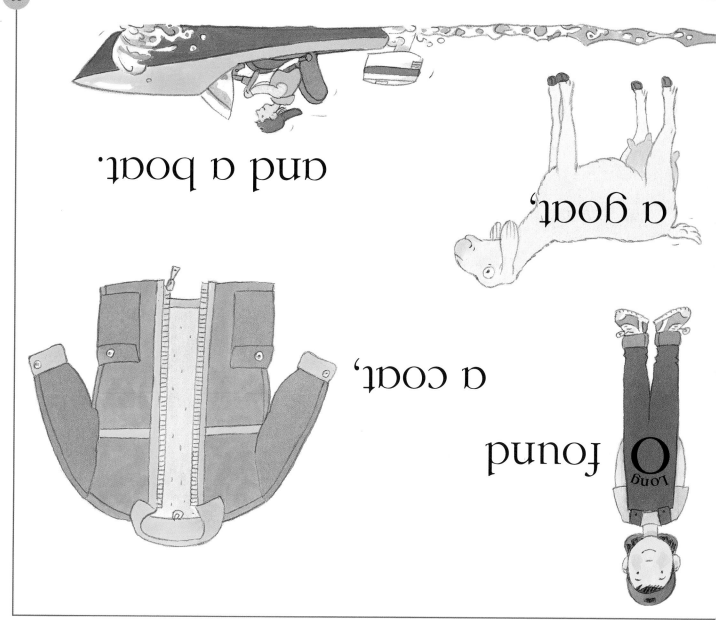

Long O found

a coat,

a goat,

and a boat.

Then she found

donuts,

roses,

"Now I win!"
she said.

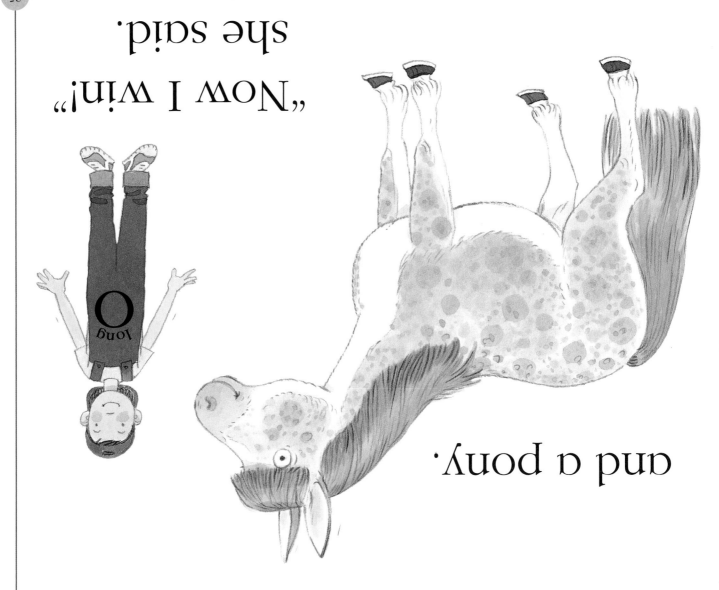

and a pony.

otter

ostrich

octopus

mop

top

rocks

fox

pot

short O

ox

blocks

Can you tell who won?

oak

pony

donuts

coat

boat

goat

oboe

roses

overalls

okra

long O

oatmeal

27

Can you read more words with short **O**?

socks

clocks

doctor

doll

dollar

ONE
THE UNITED STATES OF AMERICA
ONE DOLLAR

lock

STOP

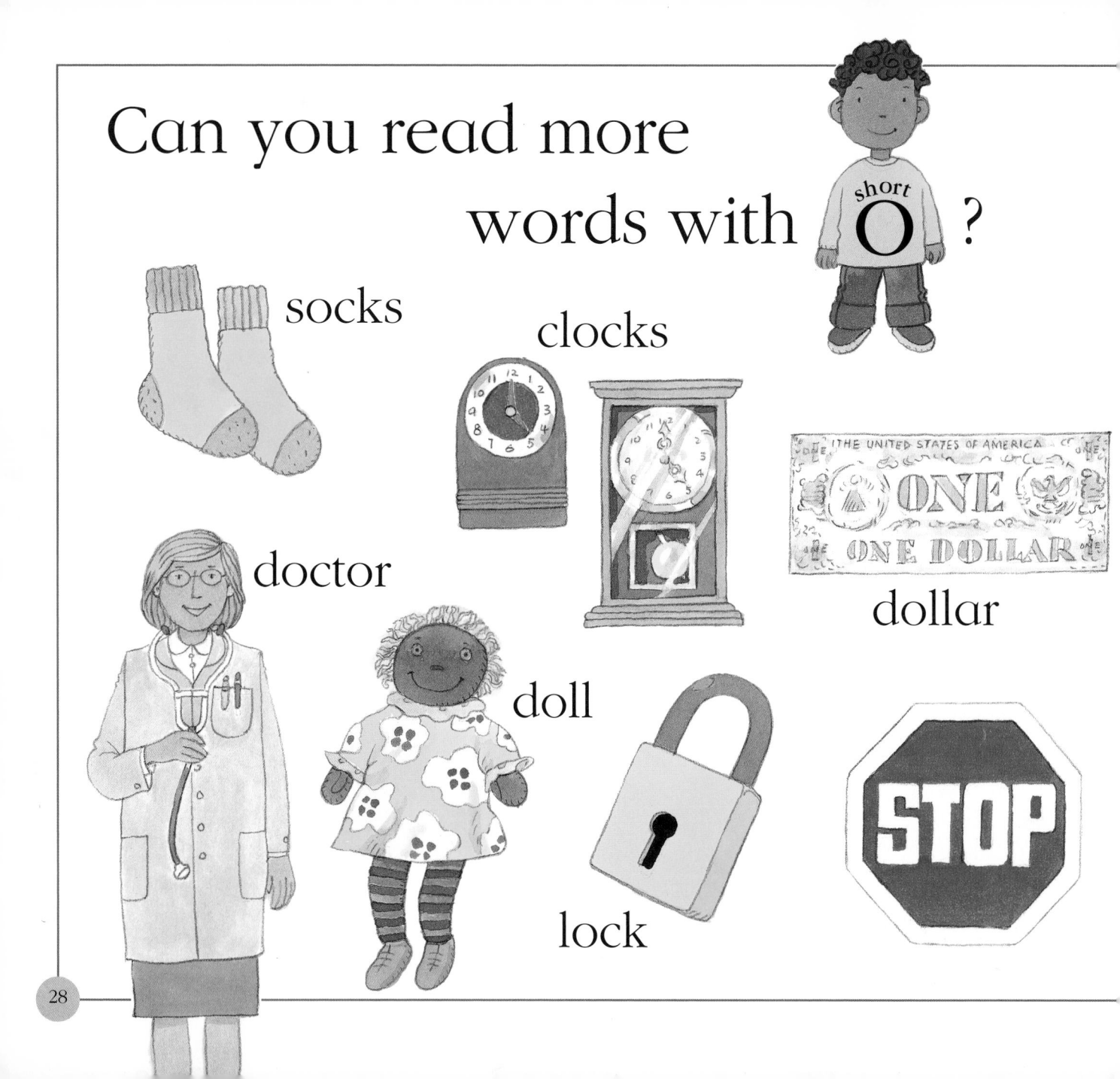

28

Can you read more words with  long O ?

rope

bow

toad

snow

crow

stove

mole

soap

Now you make up a game!

ABOUT THE AUTHOR AND ILLUSTRATOR

Jane Belk Moncure began her writing career when she was in kindergarten. She has never stopped writing. Many of her children's stories and poems have been published, to the delight of young readers, including her son Jim, whose childhood experiences found their way into many of her books.

Mrs. Moncure's writing is based upon an active career in early childhood education. A recipient of an M.A. degree from Columbia University, Mrs. Moncure has taught and directed nursery, kindergarten, and primary grade programs in California, New York, Virginia, and North Carolina. As a former member of the faculties of Virginia Commonwealth University and the University of Richmond, she taught prospective teachers in early childhood education.

Mrs. Moncure has travelled extensively abroad, studying early childhood programs in the United Kingdom, The Netherlands, and Switzerland. She was the first president of the Virginia Association for Early Childhood Education and received its award for outstanding service to young children. A resident of North Carolina, Mrs. Moncure is currently a full-time writer and educational consultant. She is married to Dr. James A. Moncure, former vice president of Elon College.

Norman Young spent his childhood on a small farm nestled at the foot of the Preseli Hills in Pembrokeshire, South West Wales. He started his artistic career as a film animator in London and then in Zagreb. Eventually he settled in Devon, where he lives beside a river that runs between the moors and the sea. It was here that he started his work as an illustrator of children's books. Norman has always had a lifelong interest in history and travel. Taking a month off work each year, he visits new places either by train or by bicycle—and he never goes anywhere without his sketchbook.